Marta Schmidt-N

My Brother is Special

My Brother Has Autism

A Story About Acceptance

Illustrated by Andreea Mironiuc

This book is dedicated to all of the children with autism who have touched my life, and my heart, over the years.

Ackowledgments

Illustration by Andreea Mironiuc
www.andreeamironiuc.com

Thank you Kellie, Jessica and Justin.

Laurie had always wanted a brother.

Whenever any of her friends at school got a new baby brother or sister, she always told her parents about it and always ended her story with, "I wish I had a baby brother."

When her parents asked her what she wanted for her birthday, her answer was always that she wanted a baby brother.

Laurie was very excited the day her mother and father came to her room and told her what she had been waiting to hear for so long.

"Laurie, we are having a baby and you are going to be a big sister."

Laurie started to jump up and down on her bed screaming with joy, "Can I name him?" Her mother and father explained to her that the baby would not be born for a long time.

They also explained to Laurie that it could be a boy, but it could also be a girl. Laurie had stopped jumping then.

"But you already have a girl," she said.

Her mother and father explained to her that it didn't matter what you already had and that Laurie would make a wonderful sister to either a brother or a sister.

When it was almost time for her mother to have the baby, Laurie's grandmother came from New York to help her parents.

When her grandmother asked Laurie to help her pick out yarn to knit things for the baby, Laurie always picked blue yarn.

She remembered hearing that blue was for boys and that pink was for girls.

Finally, the day arrived! Her parents went to the hospital to have the baby. Laurie's father said that he would call as soon as the baby was born.

Laurie sat by the phone waiting all day. It seemed to take forever to have a baby.

When the phone finally rang, her grandmother answered it and then handed it to Laurie, telling her it was her father calling.

Laurie could not contain herself and she immediately asked if it was a boy or a girl.

"Congratulations Laurie, you have a baby brother," was her father's answer.

"YIPEEEEEEEEEEEEEE!!!"

Laurie screamed as she jumped up and down, hugging her grandmother. Her father said that her mother and her brother Daniel would be home from the hospital the next day.

As soon as Laurie got off the phone, she went to her room to make a big sign to welcome Daniel and her mother home.

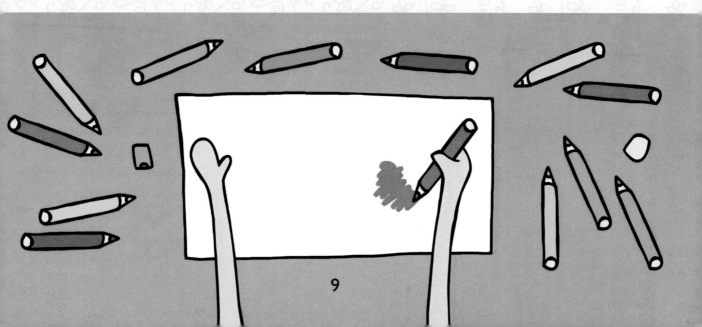

When Laurie met her brother, she thought he was the most beautiful baby she had ever seen.

From the moment that Daniel came home, Laurie was ready to help her parents with him.

She would bring diapers, help to bathe him and to dress him, and would always play with him.

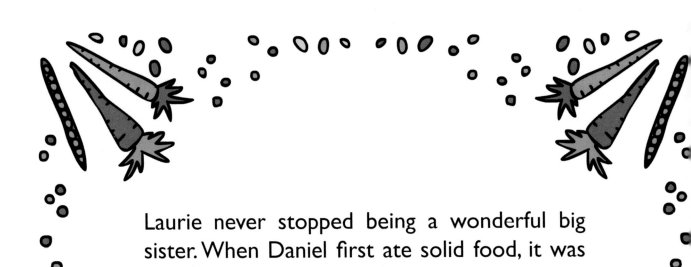

Laurie never stopped being a wonderful big sister. When Daniel first ate solid food, it was Laurie who gave him his first spoonful.

Her mother had said that Daniel might not like it, but he sure ate it and he smiled when Laurie told him how good it was.

Laurie didn't really think it was good since she didn't like squash, but lots of people did so it wasn't really lying.

Her mother called it, "encouragement." Laurie also encouraged Daniel to eat peas, carrots and spinach, but it didn't seem like Daniel needed much encouragement, since he loved everything that he tried.

When Daniel learned to crawl, it was Laurie who was on the floor with him. There was a Jack in the Box toy that Laurie would wind for hours just to see Daniel jump and giggle each time that the clown popped out.

When Daniel took his first steps, he walked to Laurie with his short, stubby little legs.

Daniel's first word was "Mama."

His second word was "Lala," for Laurie.

Soon Daniel was saying Dada, cookie, juice, milk, bottle, truck, out and banana. He seemed to learn a new word every single day.

Laurie's mother said it was because Laurie read to him so much.

Laurie didn't read very well yet, but she would sit with Daniel and would tell him stories from the books that her parents read to her.

When Daniel was about two and a half years old, the whole family went to the mall to shop for presents for the coming holidays.

Daniel seemed to enjoy the ride to the mall but as soon as they got into the mall, he began to cry. One very nice lady approached him, got down near him in his stroller and asked him what was wrong, in a soft, kind voice.

Daniel seemed to cry even harder and turned his face away. Laurie's mother commented that maybe he was not feeling well. Daniel always smiled when people spoke to him.

That was a very strange day because Daniel became more and more upset the more stores that the family went into and shrieked if anyone spoke to him.

They left the mall early, but as soon as they got to the car and put Daniel in his car seat, he seemed to be fine. Once they got home, Daniel didn't seem sick anymore.

Daniel acted the same during his father's birthday celebration. When people started to arrive, Daniel just went into a corner with his cars and stayed there.

If people went to him to say hello, he just cried and turned away. When Aunt Josie tried to hug him, he pushed her away. Laurie's grandmother took his temperature, but it was normal.

When everybody left, Daniel again seemed to be fine. Laurie went with her mother the next day when she took Daniel to the doctor.

The doctor said that Daniel was not sick.

One Saturday morning, Laurie got up very early and went into Daniel's room to read to him.
Laurie's mother got up and found her there.

Laurie was trying to read to Daniel, but Daniel was not paying attention.
He had turned his car over and was spinning the wheels.

"Why are you up so early, Laurie?" her mother asked.

"I wanted to read to Daniel because I don't think I am reading to him enough," Laurie answered.

"Why do you say that?" her mother asked.

"Mommy, Daniel doesn't talk as much anymore and he hasn't learned any new words in a very long time."

Laurie's mother looked concerned. From that day forward, Laurie's mother and father began to make a list of all of the words that Daniel was using.

It seemed that Daniel had forgotten many of his words. He seemed to whine and to reach for things instead of using his words.

Whenever the family went out, Daniel seemed to get "sick."

He would become upset in new places and with new people. He especially disliked it when strangers approached him. Whenever this happened, he would turn away or cover his eyes or his ears.

Daniel would cry now each time that Laurie tried to play with him with the Jack in the Box toy. When the clown popped out now, Daniel would scream instead of giggle. Daniel also seemed afraid of the vacuum cleaner.

Daniel would hide whenever someone used the blender. Daniel just wanted to be in his room, with his cars or trains.

If Laurie brought out blocks to play, Daniel did not want to build with them.

Daniel only wanted to line up the blocks, and if Laurie touched them after he had lined them up, he would just scream.

Daniel also stopped eating things that he used to like to eat and refused all new foods. He sometimes spit food out. All that he wanted to eat now was chicken nuggets or spaghetti noodles with no sauce.

Laurie's mother had taken Daniel to the doctor several times but the doctor said that it was a "phase" and that he would outgrow it.

He also said that boys talked later than girls.

Her mother tried to explain to the doctor that Daniel had talked early but that he had stopped using most of his words and would mainly scream for what he wanted now.

She said that Daniel didn't even point to things that he wanted anymore. The doctor had still insisted that this was normal.

One day, Laurie went into her parents' room and told them that she had changed her mind and that she didn't want a little brother anymore.

Her parents were shocked. They asked her why she felt this way.

Laurie said that Daniel didn't like her anymore and began to cry. She explained to her parents that Daniel didn't let her hug him, read to him, or play with him.

She cried harder as she told them that Daniel didn't look at her or respond to his name when she called him.

Her parents hugged her and told her that maybe Daniel couldn't hear well. They decided to get his hearing checked.

Her parents took Daniel to a hearing clinic.

When they came home, they explained to Laurie that Daniel had passed all of his hearing tests, even though he almost didn't let them complete the tests.

Daniel didn't like strangers now, or people touching him.

Her parents told Laurie that the people who had checked Daniel's hearing had referred them to a special doctor called a psychologist, to help them figure out what was wrong with Daniel.

Laurie told her parents that she was sorry that she had said that she didn't want her brother. Her mother told her that sometimes we say things we don't mean and gave her a big hug.

The day that her parents came back from taking Daniel to the psychologist, they were very sad. Laurie immediately wanted to know if Daniel was sick. Her parents sat with her and said, "Daniel is not sick, but he has autism."

27

"What's that?" Laurie asked.

Her father explained that autism meant that Daniel was different in some ways from other kids but that it did not mean that he didn't love them.

Her father explained to Laurie that Daniel now preferred to play alone, and sometimes liked to play in his own way and to repeat things over and over again.

Her father told her that there were special people who could work with Daniel and would teach them all how to help Daniel.

Soon Daniel had special teachers and therapists coming to the house. They brought toys to play with and big balls to bounce Daniel on. They played with Daniel with sand and paint and even with shaving cream.

One therapist always asked Laurie's mother to make different foods and they would sit with Daniel and help him eat new foods. They even taught Daniel to chew foods that he normally didn't like chewing.

The therapists always included Laurie in their activities and little by little Laurie learned what Daniel liked.

Laurie began to discover that she could still play with Daniel and that Daniel really did like for her to play with him, just differently than they used to play.

Laurie learned that it was important for Daniel to know what was going to happen next and that it was important for her to let him know ahead of time if she was going to make a noise, to touch his toys or to leave the room. Laurie learned to be a big sister in a different way.

It was soon time for Laurie's birthday.

All of her friends were in the backyard.

There was a castle moon bounce and Laurie's friend, Ana, was trying to get Daniel to go into the moon bounce but Daniel did not want to go in.

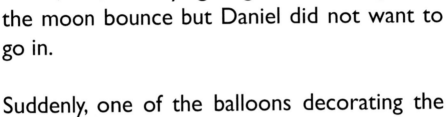

Suddenly, one of the balloons decorating the yard popped loudly.

Daniel screamed, began to cry and ran away.

Ana went to find Laurie, who was trying to comfort Daniel.

"Your brother is weird," said Ana.

Laurie looked her straight in the eye and said,

"My brother is not weird."

"My brother is special."

"My brother has autism."

About the author

Marta Schmidt-Mendez is a Child Development Specialist who has over 25 years experience working with children and families. She specializes in children with developmental disabilities.

Marta has authored numerous children's books including "My Sister is Special, My Sister has Down Syndrome," "Autism…Sometimes," "Down Syndrome…Sometimes," "Families…Sometimes," "The Barking Cow," "The Dog with the Crooked Tail," "Yip Yuck Day" and others.

All of her books deal with social issues and are geared towards helping parents and professionals speak to children about sensitive issues in a way that children can understand.

Many of her books are also available in Spanish.

Made in the USA
Las Vegas, NV
17 March 2022